Like a Compass in Her Bones

Novelette

Kristin Kozlowski

ELJ Editions, Ltd. is committed to publishing works of quality and integrity. In that spirit, we are proud to offer this novelette collection to our readers. This novelette is a work of fiction. Names, characters, places, and incidents either are the product of the author's imagination or are used fictitiously, and any resemblance to actual persons, living or dead, business establishments, events, or locales is entirely coincidental.

ISBN: 978-1-941617-55-7

Cover Design by ELJ Editions, Ltd.

ELJ Publications (Imprint)
ELJ Editions, Ltd.
P.O. Box 815
Washingtonville, NY 10992

www.elj-editions.com

For the South to my North, the West and the East,
and of course, Heaven above.

And for Aunt Carol, who tells me she's not getting any younger.

One

The small girl sobs, hiding her face in her arms. She's wearing her Sunday best: a white dress with blue edging. A dress for twirling. A showstopper.

Standing as still as possible, Emily watches the girl as the smell of the damp earth fills the space around them. The Tunnel of Souls is dark except for the dim circle of light illuminating the girl, but that's okay; Emily is used to the dark. The girl leans against something large and heavy, but Emily can't make out what it is since most of it is encased in darkness. A car, maybe? With her face buried in her arms and her body shaking with sobs, the girl doesn't see Emily standing behind her.

For a moment, Emily's heart grows heavy in her chest. There's so much grief when a child dies. So much heartache. Emily doesn't know this girl's story – she doesn't know the story of any souls she helps – but she can feel the weight of grief around this girl. Emily's throat starts to constrict with empathy. People miss this girl; Emily can feel it.

There are many emotions swirling around the souls that find themselves between the physical world and the spiritual one. Some souls burn red with anger, a heat that Emily feels crawl up her skin when she gets close to them. Others are so full of regret that Emily can feel her stomach clench with guilt. For Emily, this may be the hardest part of helping souls cross over: feeling their emotions before they depart. Few are happy. Few feel ready to leave this world behind. Even still, Emily is committed to helping these souls cross over because, she figures, someone has to do it. Someone has to lead these souls home.

Crossing children over can be tricky, and Emily doesn't want to startle the girl. Best to keep her distance and start with a small *hello*. This is something Emily has learned over the years.

Still young – not yet thirty – Emily has soft features. A wide smile, dark untamable hair, and a round face make Emily look approachable. Friendly, even. This is helpful when she encounters children in the Tunnel of Souls.

Emily takes a deep, sad breath. It's time.

"Hello," Emily says.

The girl turns but doesn't stop crying. She squints through her tears, her chest heaving up and down. She's cautious. Emily can feel her apprehension, and she can feel her fear, too. There's nothing worse than a scared child. Emily's heart aches for her. To be here alone, and to not know where to go; Emily can imagine how frightening that would be for a small child. Worse than the time Emily lost sight of her mom in the grocery store when she was young and had to run up and down aisles in absolute panic calling for her.

Emily has learned not to ask questions of the souls she's sent to help. They are already confused, and asking them questions just confuses them more, so Emily doesn't say: *do you need help?*

Instead, she says, "I'm here to help you."

When she hears this, the small girl runs to Emily with tear soaked cheeks. Emily scoops her up, and tears wet Emily's shoulder as she holds the girl.

For Emily, it's difficult not to think of her own son when she's with a child in the Tunnel of Souls. Difficult to not think of how fleeting life can be on Earth. How fragile. Emily knows she'll give her son, eight-year-old, Johnny, an extra hug when she sees him. An extra kiss. An extra bump from her shoulder to his. All things that the people who love this little girl will never get to do with her tomorrow.

Emily doesn't try to calm the girl. She doesn't whisper that everything will be okay; that will come soon enough. But Emily does embrace her, wrapping her arms around the girl. One last hug before the girl's spirit crosses over, leaving this version of home behind.

In the distance, Emily can see the door to the other side. It looks like a pinhole, like a single star in the night sky. Emily can't explain why she can see it in her mind's eye. She can't explain why it is always with her, why she can open it anytime she wants. She can't explain why she was called to do this work, the work of crossing souls over to the other side, but she was and so she does.

Concentrating on the small speck of light in the dark, Emily silently asks the door to open. She keeps her breathing steady and her focus – her energy – on the door. Slowly, the soft, white light grows. Emily calls it a door, but others might say it looks like a portal. A puddle of pure energy. An opening in the here that leads to the there.

The light grows bigger and bigger, illuminating the dark tunnel which is carved of stone and dirt. Despite being brighter than anything Emily has ever seen – brighter than a set of headlights on a rural road, brighter than the sun on a cloudless day– it doesn't hurt Emily's eyes to look at it.

In truth, it isn't difficult for Emily to open the door to the other side, and she can't explain that except to say that she thinks she gets a lot of help from those on the other side who may be called to do her job in reverse; those called to welcome the souls home. Emily thinks of this job as a calling, and she thinks that perhaps all callings are like this: equal parts difficult and easy.

When the light is big enough, Emily silently sends up a prayer for someone that the little girl knows to meet her there at the door. Sending a child off alone is not something Emily likes to do. No one should have to do this alone, but especially not a child.

As soon as Emily's prayer is sent, a figure appears just inside the light. Someone is coming to meet the girl.

As the figure walks closer to the edge of the light, Emily sees she's a dark skinned woman with thick curls and trousers ironed to a perfect crease. The woman smiles and waits at the edge of the light. Emily smiles back.

Back in her house, where Emily's physical body still rests, the door to the bedroom down the hall from Emily's bedroom opens with a slow creak. Even in her sleep, Emily is aware of the door opening. She doesn't know if she hears it, or if she just senses it as all moms sense their children stirring in the night.

Carefully setting the girl's feet on the floor, Emily peels her body away from the child's. Emily doesn't bother wiping the tears from the girl's small face; her tears will be dried soon enough and there's no need to keep the girl in the tunnel any longer. Emily points towards the large circle of light, towards the door to the other side.

"Do you see someone you know?" she says to the girl in a gentle voice.

Wiping at her dark eyes, the girl turns towards the light behind her. And without hesitation, she runs towards the light. She runs like all small children run: in a full out sprint. There is no goodbye. There is no thank you. There is just the small girl running, her black shiny shoes kicking up behind her, and just as she reaches the light, Emily can hear her yell, *Mommy!* and then she is gone.

Back in her own house, Emily's son, Johnny, stumbles down the hallway, moving from his bedroom towards Emily's.

Once the light swallows the girl, and Emily knows she is safely on the other side, Emily asks the door to close. She waits as the light shrinks down, growing smaller and smaller until it's just a pinhole again, a dot as small as a stud earring.

Without the sound of the girl's sobbing, the Tunnel of Souls falls quiet. Standing in the darkness, Emily feels the fear that gripped her chest ease, and then feels it vanish altogether. Without the girl's soul beside her, Emily is free of the girl's emotions.

A feeling of calm settles over her, one that Emily is used to in the tunnel. As long as she's alone, Emily usually feels a thick cloak of calm energy draped over her shoulders. She can't explain this either, but she's glad for it. It offers a reprieve from the heightened emotions of the souls crossing over.

This part of her night is almost over. Soon, Emily will open her eyes and find herself lying in bed, surrounded by her soft comforter and the sound of Frank's snoring. Soon, the 5:20 train will rattle past the house in the dark, it's vibration rushing through them like a spirit, shaking their bones like wind chimes. Soon, Emily's spirit – the piece of it that travels to the Tunnel of Souls during the night – will reunite with Emily's body, and she will be home.

Emily turns and heads out of the tunnel. Even as a piece of her spirit is in the Tunnel of Souls, she can sense her son moving towards her bedroom, can hear his feet padding against the wooden floorboards.

Emily hurries. She doesn't like to think that one night her son might need her while a piece of her soul is in the tunnel helping others. She doesn't know what state her physical body is in on nights like this, but she knows that she wouldn't wake up if she were shook. She knows that she wouldn't be coherent, and she doesn't want Johnny to ever have to deal with that. He's too young. He still needs his mom.

Navigating her way in the dark, Emily lets her gut lead her. She's running now, eager to allow the piece of her spirit that was away to return to her body so that she can be fully present when Johnny enters her room.

Emily rushes out of the tunnel and stops in the night air. She smells pine trees in the distance, and feels the cool damp air on her skin.

In her house, Emily's son pushes open Emily's bedroom door and rushes into the room. He crawls onto the bed.

Emily feels her body vibrate as the piece of her soul that was travelling returns to her body. Once again, she is whole.

Emily opens her eyes as Johnny curls up next to her, tucking his knees into the flesh of her belly. His eyes close, and Emily can feel his muscles already sinking back into sleep.

"I love you," he says into her shoulder as she places her arm across his skinny chest, feeling his ribs rise and fall as he breathes.

"I love you," she says, and lets herself drift off to sleep, too.

Two

Johnny's grade school is a couple blocks from their house, and Emily and Johnny walk towards it, pulling the hoods of their sweatshirts over their ears to protect them from the cool morning.

The leaves of the neighborhood oak trees burn bright yellow and orange against the gray sky, and October's crisp wind rushes past the leaves, sounding like a gap-toothed man whistling a melancholy tune.

Emily doesn't know if she'll ever grow tired of how achingly beautiful Chicago's south suburbs can be, and she hates to think that Johnny may grow to be immune to it's beauty the way that Frank seems to be. Unlike her husband and her son, Emily didn't grow up on the Southside. Emily grew up in a rusted Cutlass, zig-zagging across the United States. But not Frank. Frank is a fourth generation Southsider. His mom lives less than two miles from them, and most of his aunts and uncles and cousins are still in the area, too.

Emily spent winters in places like California and Arizona, places that don't have seasons or, at least, don't have the kind of seasons that Chicago has, the kind of seasons that let your bones know that change is on the way.

Emily likes Chicago's seasons better. She likes the cyclical nature of things, the way that birth and death circle around each other here, dancing with each other, completing each other. She's tried to talk to Frank about how she feels when summer slowly fades to fall. The anticipation of things wrapping-up, of finishing their cycle, of closing only to open again is a feeling that Emily tries hard to describe to Frank, and yet she never gets it right.

She hopes, though, that on mornings like this, Johnny can see what she sees, that he can see how beautiful a crisp autumn morning can be around here.

In the schoolyard, Emily sees a group of moms huddled together near the kindergarten doors. Their small children run through the grass, tagging each other and giggling as their moms talk nearby. Emily feels a stab of jealousy. Other moms make it look so easy. It seems effortless, the way they make friends with each other.

Johnny's been going to the same school for four years, and Emily hasn't made friends with a single parent. What does that say about her?

Growing up, her sister, Marna, was Emily's only friend. When they were little, they played with other kids at the playground, or at the beach – places where their mom let them run around while she sat nearby, basking in sunshine– but those friendships only lasted a few hours. Eventually, the other kids would go home, and Emily and Marna would follow their mom back to the blue Cutlass waiting in the parking lot.

They were never in one place long enough to rent an apartment, let alone buy a house. They didn't attend school. Instead, their mom taught them lessons under the willow trees in a park in Minnesota, or on the bed of the

Hudson River in New York. They learned to read and write with their bare legs sticking to the vinyl car seats as their mom drove them from state to state, and coast to coast. During that time, Emily never learned how to make friends, not true friends. And now she wonders if she'll ever learn. The only friends she has are Frank's friends, and it isn't that she minds Frank's friends; she doesn't. But she often wonders what it would be like to have a friend of her own.

The school bell rings so loud it permeates the red brick walls and spreads across the grounds. Johnny hugs Emily goodbye, and Emily hugs him back, wondering how much longer he'll still want to hug his mom. After last night, Emily breathes in the hug. To hold him feels like holding a lost piece of herself. Emily can't help wondering how many times the mom of the small girl from last night held her daughter tight? How many times did she breath in the scent of her hair?

Today, maybe Emily needs this hug more than Johnny does. Crossing children over to the others side is not Emily's favorite part of the job. Remembering last night drops grief like raindrops around Emily, which she shields from Johnny, moving her own energy like an umbrella above him.

As Johnny runs towards the school's door, Emily catches sight of her neighbor, Charice, who is watching her kids rush towards the building. Emily recognizes Charice by her black leather trench coat – a coat Emily loves. Emily's wearing a pair of jeans and one of Frank's oversized hoodies, which she chooses for ease as much as anything, but she does sometimes envy Charice and her bold style.

Besides Charice is another woman. That woman looks

like Charice but a few years older and with hooded eyes. She has thick braids wrapped around her head. Emily remembers that Charice's sister died of a sudden aneurysm a couple years ago. Frank told Emily about it. He mowed Charice's lawn while Charice spent a month in Atlanta with her family. Emily realizes that this woman must be the spirit of Charice's sister. But instead of looking at Charice, the woman is looking at Emily.

Emily lowers her eyes.

Some spirits, like the ones Emily helps in the Tunnel of Souls, need help crossing over. For one reason or another, they didn't walk into the light when they had the chance, and need someone like Emily to open the door back up for them. But other spirits, like the one Emily is looking at now, have already crossed over. Emily can tell because the crossed spirits feel light, and their aura is a soft gold color. Emily tries to avoid these spirits. They've traveled back to check in on the people they love. To Emily, it feels like an intimate moment, something shared between two people who love each other. Most of the time that Emily witnesses it, she feels like an intruder.

As Emily passes Charice on the sidewalk, she smiles at her neighbor, but Charice doesn't seem to notice. She's distracted by something happening at the school. The woman next to Charice, however, does notice. She reaches out and places a hand on Emily's arm. Emily turns on instinct, forgetting that she's trying to ignore the spirit. The woman holds out a book for Emily to see. It's a hardcover with thick block lettering and an image of a lightening bolt striking a tree. Emily recognizes it immediately as Charice's latest novel.

Charice is a bit of a Southside celebrity. She's published a dozen or so books, each one gaining more and more notoriety. For the last six months, Emily's seen that book being sold in every bookstore, restaurant and coffeehouse in town. There are rumors that this one will be featured on Oprah's book club.

Emily doesn't know why Charice's sister is showing her the book, but she smiles politely and keeps walking. Getting along with people is hard enough without anyone seeing Emily speaking to a dead one.

Three

At night in her sleep, Emily helps souls cross over to the other side, but during the day in her waking state, she makes soup. Today, it's split pea and butternut squash.

Jeremiah, a friend of Frank's, owns The BBQ Joint where Emily works. Frank and Jeremiah worked together at the train yard before Jeremiah quit and opened his restaurant, which has been a Southside hit for the last four years. Soups weren't on the menu when Jeremiah first opened The BBQ Joint, but when he heard that Emily made good ones, he hired her to make them for the restaurant, and people seem to love them.

The hours are great for Emily's schedule: she arrives at the restaurant after dropping Johnny off at school, preps a couple of soups to simmer, and leaves by lunch. Emily doesn't make a lot of money, but she doesn't need to, and so the partnership has been good for both Emily and Jeremiah.

Today, Emily halves two butternut squashes on a wooden cutting board beside the stainless steel oven while the split pea soup that she prepped yesterday simmers in an open pot. Arranging the squash on a baking sheet, she slides them into the heated oven.

By now, Jeremiah's usually joining Emily in the kitchen, asking about the soups and offering her some of the coffee he brews first thing every morning when he walks in the door. Without Jeremiah's deep voice bouncing across the kitchen, it's quiet. Emily flits about like a bird in a cage, hardly making a sound. Once she wipes down the cutting board, she heads to the front of the restaurant to chat with Jeremiah while the squash softens inside the oven.

In the front of the restaurant, Jeremiah sits on the barstool closest to the front door, a piece of yellow chalk in his hand and a distant look in his eyes. He looks like a man who's forgotten what he's doing. Like he's lost.

Emily holds her body still. She feels her energy sink from her head to her toes, calming her. She finds it easier to talk to people when she's calm because calmness, she finds, is something she can pass on to other people. It's like a gift she can share.

When she's calm, she approaches Jeremiah and sits two stools over. He doesn't notice, just rolls the thick stalk of chalk across his palm. The black menu board sits empty by the doors. Emily breathes and waits. Something has happened. Something is happening.

Jeremiah's trance seems to break. He remembers where he is, what he is supposed to be doing. Looking around, he sees Emily sitting with her back against the bar.

"Nomad," he says.

Jeremiah's been calling Emily *Nomad* since they first met.

Jeremiah, Frank and Emily were young and drinking at a bar near the train yard early in Emily's relationship with Frank. Over a couple of buckets of beer, Frank told

Jeremiah about how Emily was raised, how she didn't have a home, how her mom drove her from river to river and mountain to mountain, weaving their way across the states, stitching together memories out of air and sand and mud. Emily remembers a drunk Jeremiah leaning across Frank and saying with slurred speech: "But where do you call home, girl?"

Emily remembers being drunk, too. She remembers laughing and shrugging and saying: "Nowhere."

"Not a damn where," Frank says, raising his beer, clanging his bottle against Emily's and Jeremiah's. Drunk, but together, they celebrate Emily's endless wandering, her nomadic childhood. Cheers.

Back at The BBQ Joint, Emily keeps her voice soft when she says: "How's life?"

Jeremiah chuckles and pushes his dreadlocks over his shoulder. "Life is weird," Jeremiah says. "Today, life is weird."

Emily waits. Through her work in the Tunnel of Souls, she's learned how to be patient.

"Last night, I had a dream about my mom," Jeremiah says. With the mention of his mom, Jeremiah smiles, showing near-perfect teeth. His mother died unexpectedly two years ago. Emily remembers her memorial, the endless slide show of photos, the faded lace curtains on the windows of the Methodist church.

"She was standing here, right here," Jeremiah says pointing to the ground in front of him, near the entrance to the restaurant. "And she was telling me that I needed more black pepper."

Jeremiah chuckles. "She kept saying that over and over," he says. "You need more black pepper. More pepper."

"I know it was just a dream," Jeremiah says, "but it felt real, y'know. Like she was really standing here. And I know this sounds stupid, but I keep wondering what recipe she was talking about. Which recipe needs more black pepper?"

Emily knows that a lot of the recipes Jeremiah used when he first opened the restaurant were his mom's. Except for the soups and a handful of newer menu items, most of the recipes still are his mom's.

"Do you have any ideas?" Emily asks.

"Nah, not really" he says "The pulled pork sandwich, maybe? That one wasn't hers."

He runs his hand down his face, like he's trying to erase something. Emily realizes that the idea that his mom might think one of his recipes isn't right is wearing on Jeremiah's heart. Even in death, he wants to know that his mom is proud of him, and his dream is making him question that. Jeremiah loved his mom very much. Emily remembers the first year after his mom died. She remembers Jeremiah losing weight, shedding it like tears. She remembers times when she was talking to him and then realizing halfway through the conversation that he was no longer listening, that his mind had drifted off, drifted somewhere that Emily couldn't access. She knows that grief is as long as love is deep, and because of that Jeremiah will be missing his mom for a long, long time.

They sit quietly for a while as Emily tries to think of a way to ease his heartache.

"Maybe she isn't talking about a recipe," she says. "I mean, think about it. How many times does anything in a dream make logical sense? Maybe your mom was using words that you're used to – restaurant words – to tell you something, to make it easy for you to understand."

Jeremiah lowers his eyebrows, but doesn't say anything. The skin on his face folds together in concentration like hands fold together in prayer.

"Black pepper is a spice, right?" Emily says. "Maybe she was saying pepper, but she meant spice. Like you need more spice in your life. Like you need to get out more. I imagine if she were still alive, she'd look at how hard you work, and she'd tell you to take a vacation."

"When was the last time you took a day off? Went to a Sox game, or took a girl out on a date?" Emily says.

Jeremiah chuckles again. "You sound a little like her," he says. "She always asked about grandkids."

Jeremiah looks thoughtful for a moment.

"And she always said that variety was the spice of life," he says.

Emily feels something click into place, like a piece of the universe found itself in Jeremiah's words.

"Well, she was a smart woman," Emily says. "Maybe she just wants you to do something different once in a while. Add some spice to your life. You've built a great place here, and I'm sure she knows that, but don't forget to take some time for you every once in awhile."

Jeremiah nods, and Emily can see that he's really thinking about her words. She sends up a prayer of thanks for receiving the right words at the right time to help him.

"Do you think it was really her," Jeremiah says. "In my dream, I mean. Do you think it was a piece of her? Or was it just my mind remembering her, or remembering the essence of her?"

"It's hard to say, but I think it was a piece of her," Emily says.

Jeremiah sits quietly for a long time, staring at the piece of chalk in his hand.

"Do you believe in God?" he says. "I mean, I know you don't go to the Lutheran church with Frank's mom, but do you believe in God?"

Emily nods. "I do," she says. "Maybe not in a made-in-His-image sense, but yeah, I believe in God."

"So, maybe it was even Him in my dream," Jeremiah says.

"Yeah," Emily says. "Maybe."

Jeremiah exhales loudly, puffing out his lips with air. Emily knows their conversation is over.

"Alright," Jeremiah says, standing up. "What's the soup today, Nomad?"

"Split pea and butternut squash," Emily says.

Jeremiah writes the names in yellow chalk on the blackboard by the door.

As Emily walks back to the kitchen to check the squash, she hollers over her shoulder: "with extra pepper, just in case."

Four

It's easy to see beauty in the world when you get to walk an eight-year-old home from school on a beautiful day. The leaves on the oak trees already burn bright, and the maple trees will be next.

Johnny is spinning a small leather pouch in his hand. Emily knows it's filled with the arrowheads he collected out of the neighboring farm fields last spring. You'd be surprised what you can kick up if you turn over some dirt.

"Did you have show and tell today?" Emily says, nodding towards his bag of arrowheads.

"Nah," he says, "Ezra wanted to see them. He brought his so we could compare at recess."

Emily and Johnny detour around the stretch of sidewalk that's littered with broken glass, the smoky shards of a smashed beer bottle.

"Ezra had the longest arrowhead, but I had the fattest one," Johnny says.

Emily nods because it's important to nod at kids now and then.

"Do you know that Ezra doesn't dream," Johnny says.

"He says he just closes his eyes and then *bam!* he opens

them again and it's morning and nothing happens in between."

"Really?" Emily says. She doesn't say that everyone dreams. She doesn't say that it's been scientifically proven. She doesn't emphasize that Ezra must just not remember his dreams.

"And what did you say?" Emily says instead.

"I said that I dream all the time. I said that a lot happens after I close my eyes."

Emily laughs. "It does, huh?"

"Yeah," Johnny says. "Like sometimes I dream that there's a woman with wings that touches my hand and sends me magic that makes me fly."

"And sometimes I dream that our old dog, Maggie, is licking my face."

"And sometimes I dream that I'm standing outside of a large hole, like the kind that goes into a mountain that the trains can ride through, and I know that you're inside of the hole and I want to go in and find you, but I don't because it's dark and I'm scared."

Johnny falls silent for a minute, and then says: "I didn't tell Ezra about that last one."

Johnny's voice is matter-of-fact, like he's telling Emily that she should cook spaghetti for dinner, but she suddenly feels like she's on high alert. She has goose bumps along her neck, and her ears begin to ring.

"You dream about a hole in a mountain?" she says.

She tries to picture what the Tunnel of Souls looks like, but to tell the truth, she never sees it. When she's sleeping, the tunnel is just a place in the darkness. Pitch-black inside, pitch-black outside. She finds the entrance intuitively and she finds the exit the same way. Once in awhile, a small light illuminates a soul in the tunnel. Over the years, she's come to realize that those are the souls that aren't supposed to follow her out. Those are the souls that are already dead, the ones she needs to release into the light. But a lot of the time, she doesn't see anything at all. She feels her way through the Tunnel of Souls. To tell the truth, she doesn't even know if that's what it's called; it's just what she calls it.

Could the tunnel that Johnny sees in his dreams be the same one that she goes into when she's called to release lost souls?

"Sometimes I dream about the hole in the mountain," Johnny says to answer her question. "More lately."

"How often?"

"Maybe five or six times," he says.

Five or six times. He's only eight years old. Five or six dreams about the same thing seems like a lot to Emily.

Emily wasn't called to work with souls until she was twenty, and even then, she assumed it was because she had such a strange childhood. She thought that if she gave Johnny a normal childhood, he would have a normal life. Grow up normal. Have normal friends, a normal job, a normal wife.

What if she is wrong? What if it doesn't work like that? To be honest, she doesn't know how it works. She just knows that one night she went to sleep and she found herself in total blackness, and then she heard a voice say that there was someone lost in the tunnel. She offered to help, and was instinctively guided to the entrance. She found two souls that night: one who followed her safely out of the tunnel, and one who was already dead and needed to pass through the door to the other side. She saw the light from the pinhole door floating near the soul, and she asked it to open, to let the soul pass through. It did and the soul did. That was the first time, and she's been called to do it again and again, as she's been needed. Every year it seems like she's called more and more times.

"And why do you think I'm inside the tunnel?" she says.

Johnny shrugs, heading up their lawn towards their front door. "I don't know," he says. "I just know."

That evening, Emily empties the dishwasher, placing forks and spoons and knives in their individual divots in the drawer by the sink. They look like tiny, silver children each sleeping in their own bed. Down the hall, Johnny is in his room doing homework, and beside her, Frank is pacing the small kitchen in a red ball cap and sweatpants, working out the day's energy before going to bed.

"I'm just saying that eight years old is too old to be crawling into bed with his mommy," Frank says. He's annoyed. He's had a bad day and is ranting. What he's saying has less to do with Johnny and more to do with the fact that Frank is in a bad mood, so Emily doesn't say anything as she unloads the dishwasher, giving Frank space to vent. It's what he'd do for her if their days were reversed. Sometimes, Emily thinks that this is the definition of marriage.

Emily, on the other hand, is more concerned about Johnny's dreams about the Tunnel of Souls than she is about his need to come into their bedroom when he feels scared. Maybe it's the fact that she never slept alone as a kid — always coiled in the backseat of the car with Marna's skinny limbs twisted around Emily's — that makes her sympathetic to Johnny's sudden nighttime fear, but it's hard to explain things like this to Frank. Or to anybody, really. How much of Emily's life involves things that are hard to explain to others?

Emily thinks about Johnny's skinny knees pressed into her belly last night, how they remind her of Marna's knees bumping into her at night while they slept as little girls, and then as bigger girls. How when they were very young, the Cutlass' bench seat had more than enough room, but how the seat shrank as the girls grew. How there was never enough room to spread out, to cool off on long summer nights, to dream in peace.

Emily remembers the first time Frank took her home to his small apartment above a garage on the Southside. They made love on his bed. She was eighteen. The sheets were neatly tucked around the corners of the mattress when they clawed their way onto the bed. The curtains on the window were drawn because that was something you could do in a home: close the curtains. When Frank rolled off of her, he rolled so far that he had to stretch out his arm to reach Emily again, to pull her towards him. Had she ever lay that far from someone before?

She remembers how it felt to leave Frank's bed and tiptoe to the bathroom to pee, how she'd never walked naked through an apartment before. The feeling of it gave her a rush, like she was breaking the law. She wonders how stupid she would sound if she ever admitted this to Frank. How weird does it make her?

Emily's mind drifts back to Johnny's dream of her being inside of a tunnel. If it is the Tunnel of Souls that Johnny is dreaming about, is he being called to do the same work that Emily is called to do?

She hopes not. She doesn't want this for Johnny. For him, she wants a normal life. Her stomach clenches when she thinks of a piece of his spirit crossing souls over while he sleeps. How would he explain that to a wife? Would he keep it a secret the way that she does?

Emily's never told anyone that she helps souls cross over to the other side. Not her sister. Not her mom. Certainly not Frank, who's as normal as they come. How could she admit something like this to him? He'd never understand.

On the kitchen's laminate counter, Emily's phone buzzes. She doesn't recognize the number, but answering it is one way to remove herself from her conversation with Frank, or rather, the conversation he's having with himself in front of her.

Emily picks up the phone and then shrugs towards Frank as if to say: maybe I should answer this. With a loud sigh, Frank leaves the kitchen.

Frank never answers unknown numbers, but Emily does. About half the time, the unknown number is her mom calling from some new phone, either hers or one she's borrowed from someone. If Emily doesn't recognize a number, it's a toss of the coin whether or not the person on the other side will be her mom or some scammer. Some days, Emily wonders if there's a difference.

This evening, when Emily answers the phone, it's her mom on the other end.

"I'm calling to see how my favorite grandson is doing," her mom sings into the phone.

Her mom opens with that line more often than not. She wants to set her intentions right away. *I'm being a good grandma* is what she's really saying. No matter where she goes, no matter what she's doing, she always makes time to call and check on Johnny. To Emily's mom, this is important. This makes her gold.

Emily starts right in on small talk. She tells her mom that Johnny is fine, that he got the lead in the school play.

"He'll be playing Shakespeare," Emily says.

"A thespian!" her mom says, and Emily can tell she's excited. "Just like your dad."

Her mom's been doing that lately, letting pieces of information about Emily's dad slip out while Emily's on the phone. Last week was how he liked to wear a blue ball cap, and the week before was how he looked like a young Dick Van Dyke. Emily doesn't know why her mom's doing it. Why? Why now? Her mom never wanted to talk about Emily's dad when Emily was growing up, except to say that he died not long after Emily was born. Maybe it's nostalgia. Maybe her mom thinks it'll keep Emily on the phone longer if she talks about him, releasing him to Emily in bite-size pieces, pieces that Emily can chew on later.

Emily doesn't say anything. She's not sure she wants to know that her dad was a thespian. She's not sure she wants to know anything about him at all. Wondering about him reminds her that he wasn't around when she was growing up, and that reminds her of her childhood, one where her home was her mom, her sister, and the four wheels beneath their bony butts. Not exactly normal, but not exactly bad either. Emily had fun. She felt love. But it's hard to deny that something was missing. Her dad, for one. Friends, for another. Any sense of consistency or security.

Emily suddenly feels like it's been a long day. Between Frank's after-work-venting, and her mom's dad-disclosing phone call, Emily feels heavy. Maybe she doesn't ask about her dad for the same reasons she lets Frank vent without responding. Maybe Emily's gift to other people is allowing them to just be who they are without the expectation of being who Emily wants or needs them to be. But maybe she doesn't say anything because she thinks that the people in her life are like the soups in her life: better when left to simmer.

Five

Emily's been thinking about the Tunnel of Souls all day. If the tunnel in Johnny's dreams is the Tunnel of Souls, maybe Emily can tell Johnny not to go inside of it. Maybe a simple *no, thank you* from him will do.

Johnny's young. He should be running around with his friends, riding bikes or hunting for arrowheads. He shouldn't be helping souls depart this world. That's too heavy for a kid.

Isn't it her right as his mom to keep him out of the tunnel? Isn't it her duty? What is a mom if not a shield for her child?

Emily decides to talk to Johnny. To ask him about the tunnel in his dreams and encourage him to stay out of it. Kids his age shouldn't have to think about things like life and death.

Emily waits for Frank to turn on the Sox game after dinner before she talks to Johnny. It'll be better if Emily can talk to Johnny alone. Frank doesn't know about the tunnel, and explaining it is more than Emily would like to do right now.

After Emily's done loading the dishwasher with the plates from dinner, she puts a hand on Johnny's shoulder and tells him to grab his shoes. She says that they're going for a walk.

Outside, the sun has set. The houses on their street look like ink stains. The air feels cold when Emily draws it into her lungs.

Emily and Johnny walk down the sidewalk in silence, intuitively separating when they get to the spot with the broken glass. Their bodies know the way even when their eyes don't.

Emily and Johnny walk some, listening to the silence around them, watching the stars burn into the sky.

"Does the darkness bother you?" Emily asks, even though she knows the answer. When your son is small, it's easy to ask questions that you already know the answer to. Kids have few secrets at that age.

Sometimes conversations between moms and sons have to begin with something that the mom already knows if they have any hope of reaching a place where a mom can learn something new about her child. So many things about children are written on the hearts of their moms. So many things are stitched into their mom's DNA. That's where a mother's intuition comes from.

"No," Johnny says.

"When you see the tunnel in your dreams, the one you told me about the other day, do you feel scared?" Emily asks. She says it casually, like the thought just popped into her head. Like she hadn't been planning this conversation all day.

Johnny doesn't answer right away. A car rumbles past, its headlights bouncing off the sides of the houses.

"I'm not scared in my dream," Johnny says. "But when I think about it later, then I am."

This is a trajectory she didn't expect, but talking to kids is like that, especially Johnny; he's such a thoughtful kid.

"Why do you think that is?" Emily asks.

"I guess that in my dream, I know that you're inside the tunnel and I want to go in to help you, so I don't feel scared. But when I wake up, I worry about why you're in the tunnel, and then I feel scared."

This makes sense to Emily. His logical mind has a fear of the unknown, even if his sleeping mind just wants to help Emily.

"Why do you think I'm inside the tunnel?" Emily asks.

"I don't know," Johnny says. "Maybe something is holding you hostage."

"Holding me hostage?" Emily says, surprised. She never thought to look at the Tunnel of Souls from someone else's point of view.

"Who would do that?"

"I don't know," Johnny says. "A giant lizard boss. Or a dozen creepers. Or Bowser."

Emily laughs. She should have guessed that his mind would go to video games. The minds of kids are busy places.

Maybe if Emily confesses one truth to Johnny, she can ease his mind, and make it sound like the tunnel isn't a scary place. Better yet, maybe she can convince him that it's a boring place. A place he'd never want to go into out of boredom. Maybe that would be enough to keep him out of the tunnel.

Emily squeezes Johnny's small hand. Cupped together, his hands are big enough to fit a small bird inside.

A finch or a wren, maybe. Nothing as big as a robin or a cardinal. Emily wonders at this, at how a boy with such small hands can be called to do such big work. How he can be called to help usher souls to the other side. He's so young. But too young? Emily doesn't know. There aren't rulebooks for this sort of thing, or if there are, she doesn't know about them.

"Well, you're right," Emily says. "In your dream, you're right. I am inside the tunnel."

"You are?" Johnny says. His voice tilts with skepticism.

"Yeah," Emily says. "I work in there. In my dreams, that's where I work."

"What do you do?"

"Talk to people mostly," Emily says. This is barely a truth. Emily only says a few sentences to the souls she encounters. Just enough to help them cross to the other side. A few words of encouragement, maybe. Or a suggestion. If she could get away with simply nodding towards the opened door, she'd do that.

But talking is boring to Johnny. He hates the way Emily and his grandma, Betty, sometimes stand at the front door talking before Emily and Johnny leave Betty's house on days when she babysits Johnny. He always complains about how much his mom and grandma talk while he just stands at the door with his shoes on and his jacket zipped tight. To Johnny, talk is boring.

"Really?" he says.

"Really. I just go in, talk to a few people, and then leave. That's it." Emily says it as casually as she can. She tries to make this talk feel boring, too, like it's an extension of her conversations inside the tunnel. One big snooze-fest.

"Sounds boring," Johnny says.

Emily smiles. The plans moms hatch for their kids don't always work out, but when they do, it feels good.

"I guess it is," Emily says as if Johnny came up with that all by himself. "You can come inside the tunnel if you want to, but that's what's going on inside of it."

"Do I have to go inside the tunnel?" Johnny asks.

"No," Emily says. "If anyone asks you to, just say *no, thank you.*"

In the dark, Emily can see Johnny nod his head, and she knows that she's sold it.

"Okay," he says.

Down the street, a red fox races out from behind a row of bushes and rushes across the blacktop.

"Did you see that?" Johnny says, pointing. They're done talking about the tunnel, which Emily thinks is for the best. Their conversation was short and simple. Easy to digest. She feels confident that she convinced Johnny not to go into the tunnel, and the way Emily figures, boredom is as good a reason as any to keep Johnny out.

Six

The next night is Friday, and Betty asks to have Johnny spend the night. She tells Emily that she wants some grandma time.

Frank and Emily drop Johnny off and watch him race into the house with an overnight bag slung over his shoulder. He doesn't even wait for them to walk him inside. He loves spending the night with his grandma.

When Betty invites him over, she does it up right. They bake chocolate chip cookies and watch movies and play card games while chugging orange Fanta. If Emily's being honest, Betty's as close to being a perfect grandma as she can get.

Frank sighs and throws the car into reverse.

"We're not going inside?" Emily says.

"Nah," he says. "Johnny's fine. He's probably already elbow deep in a bag of potato chips."

As Frank backs his Buick out of the driveway, the door to the house opens and Betty jogs out, waving a blue piece of paper in the air like a warning flag. Frank stops the car. Sweeping up to Emily's passenger window like a bird of prey, Betty hands Emily the blue paper through the opened window.

Emily sees that it's a folded blue pamphlet. The front reads: *Vacation Bible Camp. One week during the summer. Ages 6-17.*

"Just something to think about," Betty says with a wave of her hand like a magician waving the audience into a hypnotic state. She turns and trots back into the house, closing the door behind her with a *thump* of finality.

This is something Betty does a lot: make suggestions about what she thinks Johnny *should* be doing. And, apparently, the things she thinks he should be doing involve her church.

When Johnny was an infant, Betty would gush about the babies at mass who were receiving their baptism that Sunday. She'd describe their white baptismal outfits in detail: thick satin suspenders with fabric coated buttons at the waistline for the boys. Long, wide dresses with ruffled collars for the girls. She'd pull out photos of Frank at his baptism and bring them to Emily's house when she'd visit Johnny. Betty would gush about how cute Frank looked and how special that day was for him. Emily always got the sense that the day Frank was baptized was more special for Betty than for Frank, but she never said so. She doesn't like to openly contradict Betty.

Besides, what did Emily know about church? Or baptisms? Or the meanings of religious milestones? She had never stepped inside a school, let alone a church as a child. She wasn't raised in one faith or another. She was never taught the Ten Commandments or Christ's resurrection or the meaning behind a child's baptism.

In the beginning of her marriage, Emily relied on Frank for information on what these things meant to families. She relied on Frank to interpret what Betty meant when she brought them up.

Emily wasn't sure if not going to church as a child was the same as not going to school. Was Johnny missing out? Was she?

But Frank seemed happy not to go. He never mentioned church on Sunday mornings, and when his mom noticed that his family was chronically absent from a pew she'd made sure he helped fill every week for years, she began speaking up about it. But every time Betty brought up church around Frank, he waved her off.

"It's not our thing," he'd say before walking out of the room. Not our thing.

To be honest, Emily wasn't sure if it was their thing or not. Or, at least, if it could be. But she didn't say anything. For years, she just watched.

And what she saw was that Betty desperately wanted Frank and Johnny, and maybe even Emily, to join her at the long Lutheran church off of Farmsgate Road. When Emily sat next to Betty at the dinner table and Betty brought up the idea, Emily could feel how much Betty wanted it.

One night, Emily mentioned this to Frank. He was quiet for a long time, and then he told her a story.

"Once," he said, "when I was a kid, my dad lost his job. He was out of work for almost a year. I was in middle school, maybe twelve or thirteen at the time. Too young to help really, but I did give them the money I made off my paper route that year."

"My mom worked as a waitress at the banquet hall off of 75th when they held events like weddings and city luncheons, but the hours were inconsistent and the pay wasn't good. Plus, she had to raise me."

"I was a kid, so they didn't talk about money in front

of me, but I could tell that they were sinking. Envelopes started coming with red letters stamped across the front saying: final notice. That sort of thing. And my folks stopped buying snack food. They only bought the bare essentials. If I wanted potato chips, I had to go to a friend's house. And the whole time, my mom was pulling us to church, and people were stopping us after the service to ask how we were doing or if my dad had found a job yet. Those people always told us they'd pray for us, and they always told my mom that if she needed anything, she could ask. But even as a kid, I knew my mom would never ask for help. Anyone could see that she was too proud for that."

"In the end, it wasn't the people who told us every week that they were praying for us who helped us. It was the old man next door who hadn't been to church as long as I knew him who brought over random bags of groceries. He'd pass them through the front door, grumbling about over-buying on accident. And it was my science teacher who bought me food at the cafeteria when she saw that my sack lunch went down to just the apple. And she basically admitted to being an atheist in class when a friend quizzed her about dinosaurs and how they aren't in the bible."

"Billy Beacon's family never went to church and I know because I spent the night at his house most Saturday nights, and they took me to the movies or to the water park, and they paid for everything because they knew my parents couldn't but they still wanted me to have some fun. These were the people that I saw helping my family. These were the people who opened their doors to us. Not the people that we saw in church every Sunday. Sure, those people told my mom that they'd help if she asked, but they only did that because they knew she'd never ask. It was an empty offer and they knew it."

"I didn't realize that as a kid. As a kid, I thought they were being nice when they were offering to help, but as an adult, I see how their offers weren't helpful at all. It was the people who stepped in and helped without offering that really saved us that year."

"So, I think it's fine that my mom still goes to church. And I think it's fine that she still finds comfort there. And I think it's fine that she still finds value in sitting there every week, but I don't see the value in it. I see the value in being a good person and a good neighbor. A good son. A good father. I see value in helping out when people you care about need it, but I don't see the value in going to church every week."

And Emily could feel how much that story meant to Frank. She could feel how much compassion he had for the people who had helped his family when they were struggling. She couldn't deny that it felt powerful.

After that, Emily stopped agonizing over whether or not Johnny was missing anything by not attending church every week. After that, she took Frank's lead again and focused on being a good mother and a good wife. A good neighbor. A good worker. It was why she started making soup for Jeremiah when he opened his restaurant. Helping a good person – a good friend – felt like the right thing to do.

Frank slides the pamphlet out of Emily's hands, glancing at it quickly before tossing it over his shoulder and letting it fall like a feather onto the empty backseat. For Frank, out of sight is out of mind, and the pamphlet is officially out of sight for the night.

Seven

Jeremiah's restaurant is closed for the night, but Frank, Jeremiah, and Emily are still bellied-up to the bar with a beer each and a basket of Jeremiah's homemade potato chips between them.

Jeremiah doesn't mention his dream about his mom to Frank, and Emily doesn't bring it up. Instead, Jeremiah and Frank reminisce about growing up on the Southside. Even though they didn't know each other until they worked at the rail yard, they both were born and raised here. Jeremiah is a few years older than Frank, so they ran in different circles, but the same places. They share stories about the basketball courts off of 59th where Jeremiah apparently took a ball to the chin and needed three stitches, and Frank had to scale a fence to get away from a dog that had gotten off of someone's leash and charged the court. They talk about the old movie theater near the Kmart, both of which closed almost twenty years ago.

At times like these, Emily feels a little lost. A little sad.

She admires how much of Frank's memories are tied up in where he lives.

For Emily, it is always difficult to pin down her

memories. She can't point to a place and say: *there, that's where Marna broke her arm,* or *that's where I learned to hop a fence* or *that's where I found a stray dog and fed him French fries while mom napped in the car.* The places her memories occupy are hazy. She may remember a large red maple tree, but that tree could have been anywhere. She could have been anywhere. She'd have to tug at the memory like a loose thread on a sweater to see if she could tease any more information out of it. Work backwards. Investigate the memory for more clues.

If she remembers wearing neon, then she was eleven or twelve and on the west coast. If Marna sported a pixie cut, then Emily was thirteen or fourteen and those were east coast years. Things like that.

Using everything she remembered, Emily might be able to pin down where her memory took place, but even then, the surrounding area is always muddled. The most vivid part of any of Emily's memories is her mom or Marna. They were the leading forces in her life. If the landscape is there at all, it's just a fuzzy background.

But for Frank and Jeremiah, the landscape – their hometown – is just as much a main character as the people who were there, and knowing that is what makes Emily feel like she's missing something. Maybe that's why she works so hard to give Johnny a childhood more like Frank's and less like her own. Because she doesn't feel whole. She can see how Frank has pieces of himself scattered all over town. Any story Frank tells can be corroborated by the landscape itself: *see this bent oak, this is where I ran off the road in the blizzard of 2010, smacking into this tree when it was just a sapling,* he'd say.

Until she met Frank, there wasn't anywhere that Emily could point to and tell a story. She was all wings and no roots, and she often wondered what it would take to make her feel whole. If pieces of Frank are scattered all over the Southside, then pieces of Emily are scattered all over the United States. They could be anywhere. Everywhere. How long would it take her to collect all of them? To piece herself back together?

"Here's what you need," Jeremiah is saying to Frank and Emily. He's holding his cellphone across the polished bar so Frank and Emily can see what's on the screen: a teardrop camper that looks like it's seen better days.

"A run down camper?" Frank says, confused.

"No. Well, a camper. Not rundown," Jeremiah says, snatching his phone back. "Maybe not *this* one, but something like it. A place to make your queen feel at home." He gestures towards Emily when he says: *queen*.

"Wait, so now I'm the one who needs the rundown camper?" Emily says, trying to make a joke out of it.

Jeremiah makes his signature tsk-ing noise with his mouth. "Forget the rundown part," he says. "What I'm saying is you need a place where you can go on an adventure. Y'know, get out of town for awhile. See the country. See anywhere." He finishes his beer and then opens another. "Give your girl a taste of what she's used to, man. She's been here long enough. Give her a chance to explore a little again."

This is common. People hear about Emily's childhood and they immediately romanticize it. Envy it, even. To tell the truth, it wasn't awful. Emily knew love and family and commitment. She saw oceans and mountains and deserts. But she missed a lot, too. Like safety and security. Like coming home to a warm bed. Like knowing she would sit in the same seat in the same classroom for a full school year.

Over the years, Emily has learned to keep her mouth shut about things like this, though. People don't like her spoiling their vision of a free-spirited childhood. They would rather think that having roots is worse than having wings. But in truth, Emily wonders if roots are better.

Frank looks at Emily, his eyebrows pulled close together.

Emily holds up her hands. "Hey, I didn't say anything to him about wanting a camper. I'm not even sure I know what he's talking about." She giggles then because she's not used to drinking anymore, and after two beers she's a little drunk.

The truth is that she doesn't need to leave the Southside to explore because this is the place that she's most interested in exploring. She still hasn't figured out this place. She still hasn't solved this puzzle: these borders, these structures, these deep, deep roots. Why would she want to leave a place before she figures it out? That was something she never understood about her mom.

Back at the house, Frank and Emily don't even make it to the bedroom. He pulls her down to the carpet with their jackets still on. Frank's palm cups Emily's hip and his lips find the bend where her neck meets her shoulder. Heat rises from inside of them when they join on the carpet with Emily's legs wrapped around her husband.

It's been a long time since Frank and Emily didn't make it to the bed. Emily wonders what it's about, but somewhere between the beer and the orgasm, she forgets to ask. Afterwards, they lie close together, half-clothed. She looks out the bay window. They never closed the curtains but they never turned on the lights, either. Emily thinks there's a good chance no one caught their lovemaking. On the other side of the windowpane, the moon is waning.

"We should probably move to the bed before we fall asleep right here," Frank says, his voice catching on his vocal chords, sounding like static.

"How do you know I'm not already asleep?" Emily says.

"Because you're fidgeting," he says. "When you're asleep, you're as still as stone. You don't move at all."

Eight

Emily is not called to the Tunnel of Souls that night. She's never called on nights when she's been drinking.

Nine

When Frank's mom, Betty, drops Johnny off at the house the next morning, she stays for a cup of coffee. Sitting at Emily's small kitchen table, Betty sips her coffee as it steams in its thick mug. She drinks it black. Everyone around here drinks it black and steaming hot.

Emily stands by the dishwasher, putting away dishes as she and Betty chat.

"He's a good kid, just like Frank," Betty says about Johnny.

Emily tries not to take it personally, the way Betty always attributes every good character trait that she likes about Johnny to his dad. Emily's sure Betty is not making a conscious choice to attribute Johnny's kindness or his politeness or his affinity for math to Frank and not to Emily. She's sure her mother-in-law is just making small talk, but still, it stings sometimes. Emily feels like she's being erased. Like Betty's taking a pair of scissors to Emily's small family and snipping Emily out of it. *Johnny's so smart, like his dad.* Snip, snip. *He's so even-tempered like Frank.* Snip, snip. Emily doesn't know how many snips Betty can make before Emily's completely gone. And then what will be left of her life? If someone can't point to Emily's son and say: *here, see her DNA floating around in the nuclei of his cells?* then where will Emily be?

"Did you look at the pamphlet I gave you last night?" Betty says.

Emily nods, stretching up on tippy-toe to slide a stack of clean plates onto the cabinet shelf.

"Yep," she says.

"And what do you think?" Betty says.

"I think it's a no, like always," Emily says.

She tries to be gentle. Tries not to let her annoyance show. Betty always asks for them to participate in her church functions, and Emily always says *no.* Her annoyance isn't so much at the invitations, as it is at Betty's refusal to accept that Frank and Emily aren't raising their family in the church.

And if she's being honest, Emily's also a little annoyed at the fact that Betty only brings up her church to Emily. Never to Frank.

Betty's too afraid that bringing it up to Frank will cause a fight, and Emily knows that Betty would never risk a fight with Frank. That's one change that Emily's noticed in Betty since her husband, Wyatt, passed away several years ago. Before Wyatt died, Betty didn't mind openly disagreeing with Frank, and allowing him to openly disagree with her. Betty would bring up all sorts of taboo topics: politics, abortion, gun control. But she brought up religion most of all. She never hesitated to let Frank know that she thought Johnny should be going to church every Sunday, or that he should be taking religious education classes every Tuesday night at the Lutheran church. Even if it ticked off Frank. Even if they sometimes exchanged harsh words over the topic, or if Frank left the room, slamming a beer in frustration to keep from saying something he couldn't take back.

But after Wyatt passed on, Betty began biting her tongue around Frank. She no longer brought up hot button topics, and even though the religious differences that she shared with Frank were still there, she rarely mentioned them in front of Frank.

"Johnny had some trouble sleeping last night," Betty says, changing the topic.

She takes a loud sip of scalding coffee. "I found him standing at the fireplace mantel staring at your wedding photo. When I asked him what he was doing, he said he was making sure he could find you in the dark."

"Oh, yeah?" Emily says. She tries not to let her face show her surprise. Maybe her chat with Johnny didn't go as well as she thought. To Emily, it sounds like Johnny is practicing. Like he's preparing to go into the tunnel, even though she tried to discourage him.

Betty waits for Emily to keep talking, but Emily doesn't. With Betty, it's sometimes better to say less than more. Why is it like that with some people? Maybe it's because they are better at filling the silence with their own ideas about what's going on than they are at listening to you tell them the truth.

But today, Betty sits silently at the kitchen table watching Emily unload the dishwasher. Her eyes join the bridge of her nose in sharp points, like the eyes of a hawk. Predator, not prey. There's something off in Betty's energy, and Emily knows that Betty's intuitively picking up on something. Betty knows there is more to this Johnny story. Johnny must not have answered all of Betty's questions last night, and so she's trying Emily.

Emily separates the silverware and listens to them

clank as she drops them into the divots in the drawer: spoons, forks, knives.

Around her, the air shifts. Emily can feel her skin tingle. Someone else is in the room with them. Someone from the other side.

From behind, Betty's husband, Wyatt, places his hand on Emily's shoulder. Wyatt's been dead for four years, but he likes to visit Betty and Frank and, sometimes, Emily. He likes to place a hand on their shoulders, which always feels like a very fatherly thing to do. But how would Emily know? The few years she spent as Wyatt's daughter-in-law are her only experience with fathers. Still, she likes to see him pass through their lives now and again. How he returns from the other side, she doesn't really know, but he does. Perhaps the door works both ways. Unlike the heavy, confused souls that she works with, he feels light, and has a slight gold ring around him. He's not like the souls that need to cross over. He's already moved on, but even in moving on, there's often a desire to come back. To circle around. To come home. Who hasn't wanted that before?

"What do you think Johnny meant by that?" Betty says. "You have to admit it's an odd thing to say: that he was making sure he could find you in the dark."

The coffee mugs are heavy. Opaque.

"What did he say when you asked him?" Emily says as innocently as she can. She doesn't know that she'll ever get used to the way Betty tries to pit Emily against Johnny. Or sometimes, Frank. Betty's need to double-check stories. Emily reminds herself that it's the protective nature of Betty's heart that feeds her need, the way she can never let go, the way she mothers by anticipating what comes next. How unlike Emily's own mother Betty can be. How opposite. But what's the middle ground between chaos and absolute control?

Wyatt passes by Betty, placing a thick, wrinkled hand on her shoulder. Betty turns her head slightly in his direction, like she smells something. But the moment is brief. Fleeting. Emily doubts that Betty knows what just happened. Most people don't. It's only people like Emily, the highly tuned, that sense these things with enough force to begin to see them.

"Johnny said that sometimes he dreams that you're in the dark and he needs to find you," Betty says.

Emily's chest tightens. Johnny should be outside playing with his friends. He should be tossing around a football, and going to school, and riding his bike to the rail yard to watch the trains. He should be doing normal boyhood activities, not training himself to find his mom in a dark tunnel.

Emily says: "It could mean anything. Kids say crazy things. Remember the time Johnny thought that Frank working at the rail yard meant that he could just hop a train to anywhere. He cried every night for a week thinking that his dad would just up and leave without him one day."

Emily forces a laugh that she doesn't really feel. She'll do anything to change the subject. To pull Betty off of the scent.

Betty exhales loudly, squaring her shoulders like a soldier.

"I just find it strange," Betty says. "All this talk of darkness."

Betty shudders, and then rubs her arms, warming them. "You know, evil lurks in the darkness," she says. "The bible is very clear on that."

Her eyes are like lasers, watching Emily react.

There's no way Emily can tell Betty the truth. There's

no way that Emily can say that she crosses souls to the other side while she sleeps, and that Johnny – Betty's only grandchild – may be called to do the same thing. There's no way Emily can say that Johnny's seen the tunnel where Emily works in his dreams, and that he can sense that his mother is inside. How can she speak of the spiritual when all Betty sees is the religious?

Besides, evil may lurk in the darkness, like Betty says, but Emily knows that there is goodness there, too. There is help. Comfort even. Emily knows this because she provides it to others. *She* is the goodness to be found there. Emily might not know much about spirituality, but she knows this. She feels this deep inside her bones. She is doing good work. That is why she does it.

Wyatt places both hands on his wife's shoulders as she speaks. Emily gets the impression that he's trying to steady her. Calm her, even, but he has the opposite affect. Betty flinches when Wyatt's hands settle on her shoulders, and she bumps into the kitchen table, spilling coffee from of her mug.

"I'm sorry," Betty says, lifting her mug out of the ring of coffee pooling on the formica table top.

Emily towels off the coffee. "Don't worry about it," she says. "These things happen."

"I don't know what got into me," Betty says, looking around the kitchen.

Wyatt is gone, and even if he weren't, Emily doesn't think Betty can see him. But she can sense him. If she opens up to it, Emily believes that Betty could sense Wyatt even more. Maybe even communicate with him. But Emily also thinks that Betty won't allow for that. In Betty's mind, only ministers are meant to speak on matters of life and death, so she wouldn't listen to Emily even if Emily told her what she saw. To Betty, only ministers are meant to know what happens after we die, and if Betty's minister tells her that Wyatt is in heaven, that's what Betty believes. Anything else would cause Betty to question too many things that she holds as truth, and Emily doubts that Betty would ever allow that.

"It's okay," Emily says. "Not everything needs to be explained."

And Emily doesn't know if she's talking about Betty's inability to know what made her suddenly flinch, or if she's talking about why Johnny was practicing finding his mom in the dark, but it doesn't matter; Emily believes what she said. Not everything needs to be explained.

Ten

When Emily is called to the Tunnel of Souls, she opens her dream-eyes to darkness; that's how she knows she's there. There are voices around her, people who seem to be running things, and people who, like Emily, seem to be there to help. She can hear their clothes rustle, their feet tread over the dirt, but she doesn't see them. Tonight, Emily hears these words spoken: *there's a man inside the tunnel, we need someone to go in after him.*

"I'll go," Emily says. It's what she always says.

Emily doesn't know how she knows there's an opening to a tunnel directly in front of her. It's like Johnny says: she just knows. Intuitively, Emily walks into the Tunnel of Souls, following her gut.

Emily's not alone when she enters the tunnel. She can hear others, feel their shoulders bump into hers. She always thinks that they also have souls to help. Souls to cross to the other side.

The darkness inside the tunnel is darker than outside of it, if that's even possible. Like being under a dozen blankets, one on top of the other, until the space is void of light. Until the blackness seeps into your consciousness, pulling you into it.

A dozen or so steps into the tunnel, three paths appear. Converging tunnels. Yawning mouths of more darkness. There's a calmness Emily feels in the tunnel that she never feels anywhere else. Like a coat, she feels it slip over her, and she's both in the calmness and aware of the calmness at once. It's a trippy feeling, if she's being honest, to be both subjective and objective at the exact same time, in the exact same moment.

Tonight, Emily knows she needs to move left, and so she does. It is something linked to the calmness that instructs her, moves her intuition like a needle on a radio dial, tuning her in to something she otherwise is unaware of. What frequencies are out there for her to learn? What can they teach her if she tunes in?

She is alone when she enters the left tunnel, kept company with the calmness that cloaks her, consumes her. At some point, the tunnel opens a little, bubbles into a room of sorts, a bump in the main artery. She can feel a shift in the air, and she knows she's not alone.

Sometimes, at times like this, she can still only sense the soul she encounters: she can hear them and feel them move about. Sometimes, a dim light illuminates the tunnel and she can see them. Tonight, a soft yellow glow lights the room, and Emily sees the soul that she's been called to help.

Against the tunnel wall, there's a man leaning against a bed with rumpled plaid sheets and a thick comforter cast aside. He's dressed in blue jeans and a blue ball cap. The brim of the hat shields his face from view.

Souls can be near any number of objects in the tunnel. Emily has seen some near cars or trucks, some near oxygen tanks. One was next to a large fireplace, a book in her hand.

Emily wonders if — in this moment — she's seeing a glimpse of where their body is, what's surrounding it. She wonders if she's witnessing the moment just after they die, and if the dim light in the tunnel is the light from where they are, just like the light to the other side is always present, always something Emily can see. She thinks this because as soon as the souls pass through to the other side, all of the objects surrounding them disappear from the tunnel.

Sometimes Emily thinks she should ask, but then she doesn't know whom to ask, exactly. One thing's for sure, Emily can't ask the souls. They know even less about this than her.

Emily approaches him slowly.

"Hello," she says. This is her usual opening line.

When the soul raises his head to meet Emily's gaze, he tilts the brim of his ball cap far enough back that she can see his face. The calmness she feels soaks deeper into her, penetrating her bones, settling into the marrow there. It's like the calmness knows Emily will need extra support.

The second that the man raises his head so that Emily can see his face, she knows that she's looking at her father.

It's his eyes, the way Emily's seen them in the mirror, the way she's seen them on Johnny's small face. It's the blue ball cap, the way she hears her mom's voice over the phone telling Emily how her dad always wore one. It's a pull from deep inside Emily's gut, something like an unraveling of DNA that tells her that she knows him, that the deepest parts of her know this man. It's her intuition that speaks to her, telling her that he's the man that gave a piece of himself to create her.

This man — Emily's dad — looks her square in the eyes and then cocks his head to the side, just a little, a motion she's seen Johnny do from time to time, and says: "Am I dead?"

Emily's never had a soul be so direct before. Usually, they seem confused.

"You are," she says.

The man takes a slow, loud breath like he's checking the status of his lungs.

"Are you dead?"

"No," Emily says. "I'm here to help you."

"Help me with what exactly?"

"Help you pass through the door to the other side."

He looks at Emily the way you might look at a fish you're measuring to see if it's a keeper.

"That's how this works, huh?" he says.

His words are slowed by a southern drawl. Emily tries to remember if her mom ever said where he was from. Alabama, maybe? Kentucky? Was this a piece of information that her mom let slip lately?

"What's your name?" Emily says, trying to sound casual. She's never asked a soul their name before; she's never wanted to.

"Carl Williams," he says with a nod in her direction, like he's being polite.

There's a soft ringing in her ears. A lightness in her chest, like she's filling with air. That's his name, Emily's father's name. That much, at least, her mom told her when she was young. But her mom also said that he was dead, that he'd died not long after Emily was born. *Definitely before you were two*: those were her mom's exact words. But this man, this man is old. He's older than Emily by forty or forty-five years. He's older than Emily's mom by at least twenty, Emily's sure of it.

"Carl Williams," Emily says, "where the hell have you

been?"

"I've been here for awhile, I think." His eyes move up and down the walls made with stones and covered with dirt. "Don't see no clocks, though."

He doesn't understand her question, and the reason why is obvious: he doesn't recognize her. Doesn't know who she is. Definitely doesn't know who she is in relation to him.

Emily tries again. "I'm Emily Gates."

She stumbles over her maiden name. It's been a decade since she's said it, marrying Frank when she was nineteen. She was just a girl then, a girl in a hurry to find a place for herself, to build a place if she had to: build a place out of flesh and bones, out of a man and a baby and a job.

When Emily was a teenager and found out that most kids had their father's last name, she asked her mom why she didn't have her dad's last name, too. Emily can't remember her mom's answer exactly, but remembers that it ended with a rant about the archaic practices of marriage in Western society, and it's gender biases.

But here, Emily uses her name to jog Carl's memory. To see what the name Gates will stir up, what gates it will unlock.

Carl nods. His face is tan and heavy like he's spent a lot of time in the sun. Carl has a silver band wrapped around his left ring finger.

"Are you married?"

"Yes ma'am. Over forty years if you can believe it." His smile is genuine, like he's looking through a stack of old vacation photos.

Over forty years. That makes him a married man when Emily was conceived. Dead is what her mom said about him. The story of her conception is slowly coming together. Emily bets her mom wished her dad was dead when she wound up pregnant and he wound up married. Was her mom just some girl he'd hooked up with somewhere? Did her mom know he was married before she got pregnant?

Emily fights to see through the fog of her origin story. The whole your-dad-is-dead-thing is a lie. What else is a lie? The blue ball cap thing looks true enough.

"Are you into acting by any chance?" Emily says.

"Acting?"

"Yeah, like in a theater," she says.

Carl laughs. It's the static-y laugh of a long time smoker. "No, can't say that I ever did anything like that."

Around them, the tunnel walls begin to tremble.

"What's that?" Carl says.

Emily shrugs. She's never seen the tunnel shake before. In a moment, the trembling stops, which is good because she needs to focus. She has more questions to ask.

"Just a few more things," she says. She hates that her voice sounds clinical, like she's a doctor who's taking inventory of the situation. She hates that she doesn't sound like a daughter talking to a dad, but then again, is she? He's her biological dad, of course, but where's the dad in that? Dads should be memories. They should be long hugs and short fights. They should be tired at the end of the day but still willing to read a bedtime story. They should be more than a shared mannerism passed down through chromosomes, shouldn't they?

Eleven

It's the twitching that wakes Frank. The way Emily's feet are moving even though she's lying in bed. Emily never moves while she sleeps. She's as still as stone. She never wakes Frank, but tonight she's fidgeting. Her arms are jerking, too, just a little too much. Just enough to startle Frank awake.

Frank pulls Emily to him, cradling her back against his front, molding her to him, but Emily can't be contained. Her body jerks slowly at first, but then begins to buck against him. Surprised, Frank turns her onto her back and tries to wake her, thinking maybe she's having a bad dream, or worse, a nightmare. He tries to shake her out of whatever is going on inside of her head, but she's not waking up.

"Emily," he says softly at first. "Em, wake up."

Moonlight spills through the bedroom window in sparse intervals as the clouds move past. Frank's voice doesn't help. Emily's eyes stay shut, and her body keeps jerking.

He calls to her again, louder this time. Then louder. He grabs her by her shoulders and shakes her harder, really trying now, but nothing seems to work. She's stuck in whatever dream she's having, and it doesn't look like her body likes it.

Frank doesn't want to admit it, but he's feeling panic swell inside his chest. Why isn't she waking up? What's wrong with her? He keeps shaking her shoulders calling louder and louder: *Emily! Emily!*

Twelve

"**I** lived in Kentucky, mostly," Carl says. "'Round Greensboro."

Emily thinks that's probably where he met her mom. They passed through Greensboro often: Emily, Marna and their mom. Anytime their mom wanted to cross the states, anytime she wanted to make the trek from the East Coast to the West Coast but had stayed too long into the autumn and they had to travel through the south if they wanted to survive overnights in the Cutlass.

The walls of the tunnel shake again. They've been doing that in regular intervals now. Trembling like her bones in a fever dream.

"Maybe we should get out of here?" Carl says.

Maybe they should. Emily's never seen the tunnel shake like this. It makes her think of being in a giant belly, of being pushed through intestine walls, of being digested. But she has more questions, and the only way out for Carl is through the door to the other side. Emily can't follow him there, but from the looks of the trembling walls, she can't stay here either. She's already stayed much longer than she usually does. She could have released four or five souls in this amount of time.

She wonders if that is why the tunnel walls are trembling. Could it be because she's stayed too long? She doesn't know why it'd matter, but that's the only thing about her trip tonight that's different from all the other trips. That and the shaking tunnel walls.

"Soon," Emily says.

"Tell me about your family," she says, but then she corrects herself. "Not your wife and kids. Your family before them. Your parents. Siblings."

Emily doesn't want to think about his other family. The wife and kids he spent time with while Emily was traveling from state to state with her mom and sister. She doesn't want to think about the roots he set down with some other family while she floated around, not tied to anything but a rusted car with a dream catcher dangling from a rearview mirror. She doesn't want to think about what life would have been with him as a father. She already spent too much time wondering that as a kid. But it would be nice to hear a story about her grandmother, or her grandfather. To hear what they were like might be nice.

Behind her, there's a terrible thunder, like the walls caving in. The walls shake uncontrollably for longer than ever before, but eventually, the shaking slows and then stops.

Carl looks concerned, but tells Emily a story anyway: "My father was a farmer, a tall, tan man. He grew tobacco back when that was big business. He also raised some cattle just for the family, you see. He always had chickens running around, too. When I was young, he taught me how to catch a chicken, how to stay real still and wait for it to come to you. That's how I caught my wife, too." Carl laughs, a thick static-y sound.

"Once, we watched a chicken get struck by lightning, my father and me. Saw it from the screen door during a sun shower. After the rain passed, we went out to the yard and I asked to bury the chicken. My father pointed to a young willow tree in the back corner of the property, so I went back there with a shovel and dug a small hole for the chicken. But before I could put the chicken in the hole, it suddenly bounced back up from the dirt; jumped up like it'd gotten the life blown back into it by God Himself, and started pecking the ground again. See, it was just stunned by the lightning strike; it wasn't enough to kill the dumb thing." Carl is really laughing now, wheezing on his own humor. "My dad knew that, I think. That's why he agreed to me burying it instead of skinning it for supper."

Emily laughs a little, too. It's a story she'll remember.

She's about to ask another question, a question about her grandmother, when she hears a small voice call her.

The voice is soft, like it's far away. Emily thinks of times when she was a little girl and she played with Marna in the ocean surf. She remembers how hard it was to hear each other over the crashing waves.

The tunnel walls begin to tremble again, and this time, they don't stop. The dim light surrounding Carl blinks like there's a bad connection, like the electricity is about to go out.

"Mom?"

Johnny's voice sounds far away, but Emily would know the sound of her son anywhere.

"Mom?" he calls again.

"Johnny?" Emily calls through the tunnel, back the way she came.

"Mom!" Johnny sounds relieved to hear her voice, like

he didn't expect to find her. "Mom, you have to come out now."

The walls begin to tremble again, shaking violently. Emily spreads out her arms to steady herself. Carl leans against the bed to keep his balance. He's taken to chewing the corner of his bottom lip, a habit Johnny does when he's trying to think out a math problem.

Emily feels split in two: half of her wanting to stay with Carl, to act like a kid and ask him more questions, and half of her wanting to find Johnny, to be the parent and take him out of whatever's going on in the tunnel tonight. In the end, the parent in her wins over the child in her. She can't be as selfish as her mom. She can't just do what she wants without caring about what her kid may be going through.

"Thank you for talking with me, but you have to go now," Emily says. She keeps her voice level and calm. The light that opens the door to the other side is just behind Carl's left ear.

"I'll go when you go," Carl says.

Emily shakes her head. "It doesn't work like that. I'll open up a door for you, and you can go. Once you're gone, I'll let myself out the way I came."

Carl shakes his head, a mirror to Emily. "We'll find your kid, and then I'll go."

It strikes Emily as a fatherly thing to do.

They follow the tunnel back the way Emily came. Carl's wheezing gets more pronounced the farther they go. The whistle in his lungs makes Emily think of a soup pot with a crooked lid. About halfway back, they're stopped by a pile of broken stones, large boulders that block the tunnel. Emily has never seen boulders in the tunnel before but she doesn't say anything. Carl and Johnny don't need to know that.

Emily calls to Johnny and he calls back from the other side of the seal. The walls are in a state of constant tremors now, stuttering around them, throwing them off balance.

"We'd better get to moving these." Carl's words come out in a rattle, and the walls keep shaking.

And so they do.

Emily lifts boulders the size of spare tires, the size of loneliness, the size of despair. Carl lifts boulders the size of cast iron pots, the size of regret. Johnny can barely lift anything. Youth makes him strong in compassion and courage, but not much else.

Soon, there is a hole wide enough for Emily's narrow frame to fit through. Johnny reaches for her through the hole, hugging her hand in his.

"Give me a minute," she says to the outline of his face. She can see panic in his eyes. He's scared. How could she let this happen? How could she have spent so much time in here?

Next to her, Carl leans on a boulder the size of everything Emily doesn't have time to ask him.

She touches his shoulder. "It's time," she says. She doesn't usually touch the souls in the tunnel. It feels like touching anyone else.

Carl nods either because he's too winded to talk or because there's no time left to say anything either way.

Emily steadies her breath and focuses on the door to the other side, widening the tiny light. It's hard to do with the tunnel shaking so hard. Emily spreads her legs wide to steady herself. The door grows to a great light, a sun in the dark tunnel, an eruption to someplace else. Carl raises his face to the light, like his dad maybe raised his face to the sun as it peaked over the farm. Carl's face looks like the faces of most souls in the end: peaceful.

When he enters the light, Carl turns back and tips his hat towards Emily. She gives him a nod and wonders if she should have done more, told him that she was his daughter, or told him that some part of her — the part that always wished for a dad — loved him, but she knows he'll see all that once he gets to the other side. She thinks that maybe it'll be easier for him that way, easier for him to learn who she was from the safety of the other side. She knows it would be easier for her if she never found him here, the last stop for his soul before it moved on. Easier, but maybe not better.

"Goodbye, Carl Williams," she says, but he doesn't hear her. He's already gone.

Emily closes the door, and her eyes see nothing but blackness again. Johnny is waiting for her.

The tunnel gives a violent shake, sending a loud rumble echoing against the walls. The boulders behind Emily shift again. More boulders tumble down, locking into place. The hole that Johnny and Carl helped her make is gone, covered by more stones.

"Johnny!" Emily calls.

She thinks that he must be terrified on the other side of the wall. She thinks of how his eyes looked through the hole they made, eyes like a panicked animal, like a rabbit hiding beneath a rose bush – small and scared.

Calling for him again, Emily listens for a reply but she doesn't hear anything above the rumbling of the tunnel walls, which sound like teeth chattering.

Again, she begins to claw at the boulders, trying to move them, feeling for their edges in the dark. She wishes for Carl's help. She wishes she didn't stay so long in the tunnel to talk with him. She wishes she'd never found him here. She wishes so many convoluted and contradicting things.

Thirteen

This time, the boulders are too big for Emily to move. Too many. Too big. She pounds against them with the meaty part of her fists. This has never happened before. She's never been stuck in the tunnel.

She tries to steady her breathing to keep from panicking. Johnny is just on the other side of these boulders, she tells herself. She can get to him. She can do this. Mentally, she tries to pump herself up. Rally. Try again. Her son is waiting.

Again, she claws at the boulders, pulling away the ones she can lift, but every time she removes one, the wall of boulders shifts. She's not making any progress, and all around her the tunnel walls keep shaking. At this point, it's difficult to remain on her feet, let alone de-boulder a boulder wall. And with the dim light around Carl gone, she's left feeling her way in the pitch-black.

But Johnny's still in here, and she's still in here, and the tunnel doesn't seem like it will hold up much longer. Breathing hard, Emily's about to claw at the boulders again when she feels a hand on her shoulder.

Wyatt's hand.

She doesn't have to see him to know it's her father-in-law. Like always, she feels him.

"Hey, kid," he says, a nickname he uses for her. It's something he started calling her when she was eighteen and dating his son.

Emily feels tears push behind her eyes. The shaking walls. Johnny stuck on the other side of the cave-in. Meeting the dad she thought was dead. Talking to Wyatt. The night has been too much. Emily feels her insides pulse with emotion.

"I can't get through," she says to Wyatt. It's all she can think to say. In that moment, she swears she can feel her heart break. She feels it crack like a dropped dinner plate. She always feels so calm in the tunnel. So together. But whatever is causing the shaking walls is affecting her, too. She's off-balance. Off-center. She can't think straight. The calmness that she usually feels inside the tunnel is gone, too.

"Sure you can," Wyatt says.

In life, Wyatt was always a calming presence to be around, and he feels calm to be around in death, too. He feels light, like he can absorb some of Emily's panic. Maybe Emily is just making this up, but either way, having him near her helps.

"They're too heavy," Emily says about the boulders. "I can't move them."

"Then don't."

Emily looks towards Wyatt's voice. "But Johnny's on the other side," she says.

"He's not," Wyatt says. "He's out. Everyone's out. You're the only one left in here."

Emily wipes at her tears in the dark. "Johnny's out?" she says. "You're sure?"

"I'm sure," Wyatt says. His hand is back on her shoulder, grounding her, calming her.

"He's out. Everyone's out. And now it's time for you to leave."

"But I can't get out," Emily says. The words feel sticky, like they don't want to come out of her. She feels relief that Johnny is out, but the thought that she's stuck here makes her feel heavy. Congealed.

"Sure you can." Wyatt's voice is steady. Calm.

Emily guesses that the souls of those who have already crossed over must have little cause to panic. Even if the tunnel walls are crumbling around them, Wyatt is safe. He can be out in a blink. He's not in any danger at all because the walls aren't really collapsing around him, are they? They're collapsing around her.

"No," Wyatt says, knowing her thoughts. "Not around you. Inside of you."

"What?" Emily says, not sure she heard him correctly.

"Find your way out," Wyatt says.

"But the exit is blocked," Emily says.

"Is it?" Wyatt says.

And then his hand is gone. Even in the pitch-black, Emily knows that's he's gone, too. He's back on the other side. She's alone again. The walls are vibrating against Emily's back so fiercely that she can feel her insides shake, like her bones are humming. Strangely, it makes her feel lighter, like her body is shedding the pieces that it doesn't need, like scraps of herself are flaking off and falling to the floor.

She stands.

Intuitively, Emily knows that the blocked tunnel is to her right. Closing her eyes, she tries to steady her breathing. Instead of calling to Johnny again, she tries to reach out to him intuitively — instinctively — to see if he really is gone from the tunnel. She reminds herself that she knows when he wakes in the middle of the night even before he comes to her room. She reminds herself that even in her sleep, she can feel when he's awake and when he's asleep, when he's in his bed and when he's not. Drawing on that feeling, that primal connection, she reaches out for him, and finds with relief that Wyatt is right: Johnny's gone. If he were near her in the tunnel, she would feel it; she knows she would.

Emily places her hands against the boulders. The stones vibrate against her skin. They feel heavy. Solid. What was it that Wyatt said when she said that the exit was blocked? *Is it?*

Emily thinks for a moment. Every time she's entered the tunnel, she's used her intuition to lead her. Her inner compass. The feeling in her gut. And every time she's left, she's done the same. So why not now?

Emily ran in this direction because she heard Johnny calling for her. She assumed that this was the way out, and maybe it is, but maybe it's not the only way out. Maybe there's another way. Maybe there's lots of other ways. Emily's never explored the tunnel; she's always just gone in and come back out.

Again, Emily tries to steady her breathing. She needs to know which way to go. She needs to find her way out, find her way back to Frank and Johnny, find her way home.

Emily breathes deeply, trying to call the calm that she usually feels inside the tunnel back to her. She needs it to think straight. To feel straight.

Left.

Emily can feel her body want to move towards her left.

And so she does.

Stumbling in the dark, Emily moves through the shaking tunnel like a marble in a pinball machine, following her own momentum. The calm feeling begins to settle over her again. It doesn't feel like the thick coat that it usually does; it feels more like a thin jacket. But still, it's there. It's back. Emily draws on that calm feeling, using it to fuel her intuition.

She gets to another break in the tunnel and she slows down. She reaches deep inside of herself, trying to sense which way to go.

Left.

She feels it in her gut, in the soft squish below her rib cage. She turns and keeps moving.

The darkness makes her think about walking outside with Johnny, of talking with him in the dark to make sure that he wasn't afraid. If she had the ability to keep him away from the Tunnel of Souls, would she? Before tonight, she would have said the tunnel was safe. She'd never felt scared or nervous or upset inside the tunnel. It didn't matter that she worked with souls who were departing this realm, and that many people would be freaked out by that — people like her mother-in-law, she guessed. But Emily wasn't freaked out by that. She'd felt helpful and needed. She'd felt like she was a piece of a puzzle that she couldn't quite see, but participated in because she believed she'd see the whole of it one day. She'd never felt afraid before, but tonight, she feels the beginning of fear creep around her edges like a sheet of paper catching fire. She feels the slow burn of fear eating away at her, trying to separate her from the thin layer of calm that rests on her shoulders.

Should she feel afraid? She'd never thought to before; she'd always went on feeling. On intuition. On gut instinct. That was her mom's DNA in her. But when Emily adds the element of intellect, she thinks that maybe she should be afraid. Maybe there is a reason the tunnel is collapsing. Maybe she can get stuck in it; maybe she could have been stuck in the tunnel any night that she entered it. Should she have said no when she was first asked to go into the tunnel years ago?

Emily's fear propels her. She moves faster. Her legs feel like noodles over the trembling tunnel floor, but she keeps going, sometimes pitching over and slamming against one wall or another. She keeps moving until something inside of her screams stop! And she does, just before she slams into a wall.

Reaching out her hands, Emily feels the space in front of her body. It's a wall of boulders just like the one that fell between her and Johnny, blocking her. The stones vibrate beneath her palms, and they rattle like teeth clanking together.

Emily feels panic well up inside of her. Any sense of calmness that she ever felt in the tunnel is gone now. All that's left is fear gnawing at her. Her mind is spinning. She can't think. Her lungs are constricting. She can't breath. Her mind tells her that she's trapped. Her mind tells her that she's stuck, that she'll never see her family again.

Between the cave walls around her and her mind inside of her, Emily is crumbling. Emily drops her hands to her sides. Her body feels hot.

She considers turning back, finding a new way, but she doubts it will work. If all of the tunnels haven't collapsed yet, they will soon. The ground shakes beneath her feet, and the walls around her tremble.

Fourteen

The door to Frank's bedroom opens with a panicked, creaking sound.

"Johnny, go back to bed," Frank says barely looking at the boy. All of his focus is on Emily's sleeping, shaking body. She's almost convulsing now, her limbs striking out at rough intervals, sometimes kicking, sometimes slapping the bed. To Frank, it looks like her body is in distress, but he doesn't know how that can be. He doesn't understand what is going on right next to him.

"Stop it," Johnny says to his dad who is shaking Emily, trying to wake her.

Frank doesn't listen. Johnny's face is wrapped in tears. He's choking on his sobs.

"You're making it worse," Johnny yells at his dad.

Kneeling over his mom, Johnny shoves his dad using both small hands. It's not so much Johnny's force but the fact that he shoved him at all that stops Frank.

"She's not gonna wake up," Johnny says. "She's stuck in the tunnel."

"What?"

"She's stuck in the tunnel," Johnny says.

Outside the bedroom window, the branches of the oak tree claw through the night air. "I was just there. She's inside."

"Inside where?" Frank says.

"Inside the tunnel," Johnny says. He's choking on the words like smoke, like panic, like too-little-air.

To Frank, Johnny suddenly looks older, far older than eight years old. How did that happen?

"I tried to help her," Johnny says. "I found her and I tried to help her, but I couldn't stay any longer. I got pulled out. I left her there alone."

Johnny's voice shrieks into the room like a trapped bird flying around in a panic. He's crying so hard he can hardly speak. His eyes are swelling from the force of his tears.

Johnny's shaking on the bed, rocking back and forth. Frank's not sure he is hearing him correctly, but it sounds like Johnny is saying: *I tried to help her, Dad. I tried. I tried.*

Fifteen

Emily thinks about Johnny. She hopes that he's home in bed, that he thought his time in the tunnel was all a dream, or that he crawled into bed beside her, not noticing that she didn't wake when he opened her bedroom door. When Emily closes her eyes, she can almost feel Johnny's small frame pressed up against her just like Marna's body used to be when they were kids.

And somewhere in the gray matter of her brain, her memories take root and begin to spread. She thinks about her mom driving barefoot with the windows open, and Emily feels her body sway against the bench seat as they cross the country again and again. She thinks of the way Frank grabs her hand while he drives, how he's always reaching for a physical link between the two of them.

Her memories spread like tree branches, pushing their way toward the surface of her mind, shoving her fear aside, and Emily realizes that she has never felt afraid in the tunnel before because there's nothing to be afraid of in the tunnel.

What was it that Wyatt said when Emily thought that the tunnel walls were collapsing around her? *Not around, inside.*

She had never thought much about the Tunnel of Souls before, about it's construction, about it's pathways. But it has to begin somewhere, and it has to end somewhere.

What if it starts inside of her? The tunnel only began to shake after Emily had spent a long time talking to her dad. What if it's not the tunnel that's collapsing, but Emily's link to it? What if she just spent too much time inside of it? Too much energy? What if the tunnel is like the door to the other side? What if Emily is the battery that fuels the whole thing?

If that is true then Emily can stop the tunnel from collapsing. She just needs to concentrate.

Emily takes a deep breath. She tries to focus.

She takes one breath in and lets one breath out, pushing the air between her lips with purpose, with force. She can feel the fear that had been nibbling inside her fade away, and she can hear her mind begin to quiet.

She calls the calmness back to her, inhaling and exhaling in steady streams.

Slowly, she lifts her hands to the boulders blocking her way. If she can open up a door to the other side, she can move these boulders. She tells herself this.

She can.

She breaths in, breaths out.

The trembling around her begins to slow.

Emily can feel her body building energy. She feels like a balloon being filled.

As Emily breathes, the ground beneath her feet steadies. The tunnel walls grow still. It's only the boulders in front of her that keep shaking, the boulders beneath her hands. Emily concentrates. She draws her energy towards the boulders blocking her way, and the boulders shake fiercely.

With a great rumble, the boulders begin to unhinge. One moves, and then another, and another. They shift and fall, tumbling one over the other, the top ones rolling to the bottom. Dust rises into the air in a thick cloud.

To keep from being pummeled, Emily jumps back and waits for the boulders to fall. She waves her hand in front of her face to keep from inhaling the dust.

When they stop, she is faced with a pile of boulders, but at the top of the pile is enough room for Emily to crawl over and out.

Wasting no time, Emily begins scaling the boulders, which roll beneath her weight, threatening to topple her. She crawls as fast as she can, clawing her way over the rubble, navigating her way back to her body, back to Frank and Johnny and the home she's spent years stitching together. Back to the Southside, to their tiny kitchen table, to walking Johnny to school.

Finally, Emily reaches the other side of the pile. She stands and begins running again.

The tunnel floor pitches upward and Emily follows up, up, until she bursts out of the tunnel and into the night air. She can feel the cool openness around her. The air shifts and she can feel the calmness that she called to her releasing, lifting away. She takes a deep breath, fills her lungs with air, and pulls herself out of sleep.

Sixteen

Hand in hand, Emily and Johnny follow the sidewalk towards Johnny's school. Above, a gaggle of geese pass in the sky, their V shape like an arrowhead, like a compass needle pointing their way. Emily and Johnny are low on sleep, but that doesn't bother Emily. They are safe. They are happy. Emily never realized just how valuable those two things were. She'd spent so much time contemplating how to be normal that she'd never considered how lucky she was just to be safe and happy. She'd never before thought that maybe that was enough. But today the trees are filling the sky with their bright colors, and the chilled morning air is reminding them that they are alive, and for Emily, that is more than enough.

Last night, when Emily finally woke up, Frank and Johnny were both kneeling beside her on the bed, their eyes wide and their breathing heavy. Johnny hugged Emily tight, pressing his arms deep into her flesh, and then Frank piled on, his thick arms encircling them both, making Emily feel safe and grounded and home.

She hadn't thought about it until that moment, but she

suddenly realized that she was home. Not home in the sense of being inside the house where she lived, but home in the sense that she was with the two of them, and that they were her home. She realized that home wasn't the mowed lawn and the curtains and the dishes in the cabinets; it was the binding together of people. It was the family that she had created. All these years, Emily had been searching for a home, but now she realized what her mom knew all along: home wasn't a place. It was a creation. And Emily had created one for herself.

Of course, there are still things to do. There's a long talk that Emily will have to have with Frank. A talk where she admits to what she does while she sleeps, where she goes, who she helps. A talk about her dad, and her mom. But Emily knows that she has time for all of that. Time is a powerful gift, and Emily's happy to have it.

Johnny is quiet on the way to school. He worries his bottom lip the way he does when he's working through a problem. For the first time in her life, Emily looks at her son and thinks that he looks like her dad. That's when Emily realizes what a gift last night was. Her chest locks a little. Maybe she didn't know her dad very well, but at least she got to spend a little bit of time with him. Got to ask him a few questions. Got to unravel the truth about him just a bit. It wasn't everything, but it was something and Emily feels her chest lighten at the thought, an untying of emotion around her heart. Her dad is gone now, but her memory of the time they spent inside the tunnel is still there. She'll always have that.

"Can I ask you something?" Johnny says as they approach the school.

"Sure," Emily says, squeezing Johnny's small hand as they walk.

"How do you know where to go in the tunnel?" Johnny asks. "It's so dark in there."

It's a solid question. An honest one.

Emily remembers hearing Johnny's voice call for her inside the tunnel last night. She remembers the way her stomach dropped at the sound of panic in his voice. But she's beginning to think about it differently. She's beginning to see that what Johnny has been given is a gift. It's a gift for him to be able to help others in the way that she does. Just like Frank is gifted at caring for his community, and Jeremiah is gifted at feeding others, and Betty is gifted at teaching, Emily and Johnny are gifted at helping souls when they need it the most. And instead of convincing him to shy away from that, perhaps she should help him lean into it. Grow into it. Learn it. And maybe this is the start of that.

Before they left for school that morning, Emily talked to Johnny about leaving the tunnel the night before. Johnny told her that he didn't mean to, that he didn't want to leave her there. His breath was heavy when he said it, catching against the sobs that were beginning to bubble inside of him while he talked. Emily rubbed circles on his back.

Johnny said that one minute he was next to the boulders, waiting for her to squeeze through the hole they made, and the next minute something lifted him off the ground and flew him out of the tunnel.

"You mean carried you," Frank said from the kitchen table where he was listening.

"No," Johnny said. His words were strong. "Flew me."

Even at his young age, Johnny is sure of himself. He's already starting to follow his intuition in ways that other people never do. After all, that's how he got into the tunnel last night. That's how he found Emily.

Emily contemplates Johnny's question, trying to think of a way to describe how she finds her way in the tunnel. Perhaps being a shield isn't the best thing she can do as his parent. Perhaps giving him the skills that he'll need to grow and learn is a better way.

Emily considers how she can teach Johnny to find his way in the dark. How can she describe the pull in her gut? The knowing deep inside of her like a compass in her bones that she follows without thinking? What words will help him navigate the tunnel? What words will help him navigate this world?

Emily would like to explain it better and she's not sure if what she's describing makes any sense, but what she says is: "I go where my gut tells me to, and I know when I'm heading in the right direction because it feels like going home."

That seems enough for Johnny. He hugs her, hanging onto her waist for a little longer than usual before running into the school.

Standing beside Emily is Charice, and beside Charice is the spirit of her sister, the woman with the braids circling her head. The woman holds Charice's book towards Emily, and opens to the dedication page. The page reads: *for Biggie, who is in every word.*

And suddenly Emily understands.

Emily smiles at Charice. "Walk you home?" she says.

Charice looks surprised but she nods. They've been neighbors for years but have never walked to or from school together. As they fall in step together, Charice's sister trails behind them.

"I've seen your book around town," Emily says breaking the silence. "The new one."

Charice laughs. "Yeah, everyone's being really supportive."

"As usual," Emily says, smiling.

"As usual," Charice agrees.

"You wrote it for your sister, right?" Emily says.

Charice catches her foot on a lip in the sidewalk and stumbles briefly.

"Yeah," she says. "How did you know that?"

"The dedication: *for Biggie*. It's what you called her," Emily says. She doesn't know how she knows this, she just does. It's as if Charice's sister is feeding Emily the information.

"Nobody knows that but my sister and me," Charice says.

"What if I tell you that I can see your sister." Emily says. "And that she wants me to tell you that she's read your book and she's really proud of you. And that she misses you."

Emily is holding her breath, fighting the panic that's threatening to bubble over. Her ears burn with blood. Maybe Charice will punch her. Or spit in her face.

Charice stops. Her eyes fill with tears.

Without warning, she reaches for Emily and pulls her to her chest, hugging her.

"I would say: thank you," Charice says. "Thank you."

Emily releases the air she's been holding, and all around them leaves fall from the trees.

Acknowledgements

To Steve, who watches me write every day at the kitchen table; to Helen, Warren and Edison, who always check my plot points; to my parents, Bob and Gayle, who always knew I'd write a book one day; and to Bob, Richard and Angela, who spent many hours walking to the library with me as a kid, I would like to offer a soul-bellowing, realm-shattering thank you. I would never have written anything without your support. I love each and every one of you.

I would also like to offer a thank you to Konrad Wardh for tolerating me as a critique partner; Michael Alperstein for reading a draft; the Pacific & Mountain Writers & Healers writing group for allowing a central time zone citizen into your circle of light; Denise Correll for teaching me to be a great listener of Spirit; and my Thursday night crew, who encourage me to keep my metaphysical life front-and-center in all things, even my writing. Thank you to all of you: Conrad Rodriguez, Allison Poole, Gina Young, Jen Lansink, Jody Goddard, Jolena Long, Kate Trotter, Kathryn Woodfine, Kim Pacitto, Summer O'Keefe, Mercedes Lahaie, Nathalie Rodriguez, and Catrice Jaramillo. You are all beautiful souls.

A submission call for a novelette is not something you see every day. Thank you to ELJ Editions for believing in this form, and for all of the hard work you did to format and publish this book. Thank you, as well, to Ariana Den Bleyker for believing in this story, designing the cover, and holding my hand through the publishing process. I appreciate every second you spent on Emily's story.

About the Author

Kristin Kozlowski lives and works in the Midwest, US. Some of her work is available online at *Flash Frog, matchbook, Vast Chasm, Pidgeonholes, Lost Balloon,* and others. Her piece from *Cease, Cows,* "Salty Owl," is included in *The Best Small Fictions Anthology 2021,* "What's the Opposite of Thief?" from *The Birdseed* was nominated for *Best MicroFiction 2022,* and "Behind Closed Doors" from *Vast Chasm* was nominated for *Best Microfiction 2023.* For her upcoming publications, please visit her website at kristinkozlowskiwrites.wordpress.com. If you tweet or use Instagram: @kriskozlowski.

Made in the USA
Monee, IL
01 March 2023

28988105R00052